CONTENTS

D0245082

Nardole's Codebreaker

Use this key to decipher the extra facts Nardole has added to each of Bill's assignments!

A	B	C	D	E	F	G	H	I	J	K	L	M

N	O	P	Q	R	S	T	U	V	W	X	Y	Z

Introducing...
The Doctor

YOU'RE LATE!

KNOW WHAT YOU'RE THINKING: 'HOW CAN I BE LATE FOR A BOOK? IT'S A BOOK! A FIXED POINT IN TIME AND SPACE!' WELL, I'M A TIME LORD, AND I SAY YOU CAN BE LATE FOR ANYTHING, INCLUDING A BOOK. AND YOU ARE DEFINITELY LATE.

Since I saw you last, there have been a few changes. The main one is that I've got a job. Me! A job! Hilarious, isn't it? I'm a university lecturer, which is marvellous and exactly what want to be doing. I certainly don't sneak off and have adventures when nobody is looking. That would be very naughty.

I've been doing this job for a while now. Can't remember exactly how long. Might be since last Christmas, but I've heard a rumour it's more than seventy years. There's a slim chance it could be both at the same time! My life is often funny like that.

This is my office. Swanky, eh? I asked for one on the first floor, to make life a bit harder for any Daleks who might turn up unexpectedly. Plus, I like the exercise – it's good for my hearts!

That's the TARDIS, of course – short for Time And Relative Dimension In Space. I use it for travelling anywhere in the universe at any time, but if anyone here asks I tell them it's a cupboard for keeping umbrellas in.

I see you've already met Nardole. Mostly he answers the door, makes the tea and helps keep me on the straight and narrow – which, as anyone who's met me will know, is a tricky job. Occasionally he helps me out with certain other mysterious matters, too.

What do I keep in my Vault underneath the university? Just a load of junk. Christmas decorations, a rusty bike, old copies of the *Beano* . . . Oh, and a very dangerous thing that I promised to stay with on Earth and guard for a thousand years. Nothing for you to worry about!

You don't fool me, though. I know why you're really here. You've heard I'm taking on new students, haven't you? Well, I might be – but only the very best and bravest, like Bill Potts. So read this book carefully, because there WILL be a test at the end, and I don't take on anyone who gets less than top marks.

Before we start, you'll need an ID card so you can come and go at the university without attracting suspicion. Fill this in and stick on a picture of yourself. (Serious photographs only, please. No dog-face filters.)

UNI ID

NAME:

AGE:

PLANET OF ORIGIN:

SPECIAL POWERS:

APPROVED BY: *The Doctor*

UNI ID

Place your photo here

JOB APPLICATION FORM

SURNAME: *Doctor*

FIRST NAME: *The*

AGE: *Over 2000. (Technically it could be four and a half billion, thanks to all the time I spent chipping away at that Azbantium wall, but I prefer not to count that.)*

MARITAL STATUS: *Widower*

ADDRESS: *The TARDIS*

TIME AT THIS ADDRESS: *Yes*

PREVIOUS ADDRESS: *Flat 40, Singing Towers View, Darillium*

TIME AT THIS ADDRESS: *24 years*

COUNTRY OF ORIGIN: *More of a planet, really. Gallifrey, previously in the constellation of Kasterborous, galactic coordinates 10-0-11-00:02, now at the end of the universe, give or take a star system.*

PREVIOUS EMPLOYMENT:

1970–75: Scientific Advisor, Unified Intelligence Task Force (UNIT)

2014: Caretaker, Coal Hill School, London

2014–PRESENT: President of Earth

REASON FOR APPLYING: *To pass on my unlimited knowledge of absolutely everything to a new generation. (Also, I need somewhere to easily guard a top-secret vault, no questions asked.)*

Regeneration!

WHEN YOU'VE LIVED AS LONG AS I HAVE, IT'S ONLY NATURAL TO GET THROUGH A FEW DIFFERENT FACES. TIME LORDS CAN PRACTICALLY LIVE FOREVER, BARRING ACCIDENTS. UNFORTUNATELY, I LIVE THE KIND OF LIFE WHERE ACCIDENTS OCCUR QUITE REGULARLY . . .

Luckily, if anything really bad happens and my body dies, I can regenerate. New face, new body, but still the same Doctor underneath. Neat, eh?

The rule used to be that each Time Lord could only regenerate twelve times, but I've never been one for following rules, so I've been able to go beyond the limit.

There have been fourteen of me so far – although two of them looked the same, because one was so pleased with himself that he kept the same face.

Some intergalactic records state that I'm the Twelfth Doctor, which is both right and wrong, depending on your point of view. Confusing! But everything about me is confusing, so don't worry about that too much.

When I change, there's usually a massive eruption of energy, so if you see me starting to glow stand well back. I sometimes let out a bit of energy to help people in need, or just to show off, which means I'll probably end up without a nose at some point. I'll cross that bridge when I come to it.

Eventually, I'll have to give up this face, and then there will be a new Doctor out there in the TARDIS, fighting monsters and saving people. When that happens, I hope you won't forget me. I mean, look at these eyebrows. Who could forget eyebrows like these?

Regeneration in the Doctor's words . . .

> I don't suppose there's a need for a doctor any more. Make me a warrior now.

> Wearing a bit thin. I hope the ears are a bit less conspicuous this time.

> I might have two heads. Or no head! Imagine me with no head.

Five Spectacular Regenerations

1. The Eleventh Doctor's regeneration was so explosive, he used the energy to take out the whole Dalek fleet.

2. Friendly old Professor Yana got a shock when his memory came back and he realised he'd been the Master all along!

3. Amy Pond was freaked out when her best friend, Mels, started to glow and change – especially when she turned into Amy's daughter, River Song.

4. The General was an old man when he started to regenerate, and a young woman by the time she was finished.

5. The Tenth Doctor held off his regeneration for so long that when he finally let go the mighty force wrecked the TARDIS.

Everything I am dies. Some new man goes sauntering away. And I'm dead.

Everything you are, gone in a moment, like breath on a mirror. Any moment now, he's a-comin'.

We're on Gallifrey – death is Time Lord for man flu.

Introducing...
Bill Potts

Okay, where do I start?

I was at work one day, shovelling chips in the university canteen, when this guy appeared. Bobble hat, duffel coat, and he was squeaking as he walked! He said the Doctor wanted to see me and I froze, because I knew why.

I'd been sneaking into his lectures for ages. I'd heard the students talking about him. Said he knew everything about everything, and I thought, 'Well, I don't know much about anything, so I want a bit of that.'

So there I was, sat in front of the Doctor, thinking I'm going to get sacked or charged tuition fees or something. But he said he was going to be my personal tutor! All I had to do was turn up every night and ace every assignment.

What he forgot to mention was that I'd be travelling through time and space, seeing the best and the worst of the universe and everything in between. I mean, when was I supposed to do my homework?

This is my mum. She died when I was young, but I still talk to her all the time. I've always hoped she can hear me somehow, and that she's looking out for me. We'd never have sorted out the Monks if I hadn't believed that. We only got rid of them because she's still in every corner of my mind.

Once I started studying, it was time to move out of my foster-mum Moira's place. I found an amazing house, but it turned out to be infested with space-lice, and then there was an ancient wooden lady living in the tower, and then the whole house fell down. So I moved back in with Moira.

Some days, the Doctor says he's only here to do as the human race tells him, meaning it's up to me to make tough decisions. Other days, he gets angry when I don't do what he says. Usually, one of us manages to do the right thing. But he's seen so much death and destruction, and I'll never get used to that . . .

The Doctor asks...

What did Bill first think the TARDIS looked like?

A: A kitchen

B: A garden shed

C: A bathroom

I met this girl called Heather. She seemed sad, but I liked her. I thought she was playing it cool when I asked her about the star in her eye.

But she'd actually been taken over by living fluid from an alien ship! It wanted to get away and so did she. A perfect match!

Heather liked me, so the part of her that was still Heather made the alien part chase me across the universe.

It seemed like the r Heather was gone forever, and the Doc wanted to wipe my mind so I'd forget it But then he change his mind. I'm really he did.

Bill's Assignment: The Daleks

YOU ARE AN ENEMY OF THE DALEKS! EXTERMINATE!

Thing with tentacles

Sucker (ran out of guns)

Energy gun

Keeps his phone and keys in here?

Nice try, Bill – they're sensor globes!

INFO DUMP

What is a Dalek? I asked YOU that, Doctor! You told me it was 'just a Dalek'. Don't get smart with me, Bill. Hold on, WHAT? How did the next question just change like that? Because I'm really very clever. Now, come on – you know this. Okay, okay. You said something about 'the deadliest alien war machine ever devised'. Very good. Where do Daleks come from? A corridor. Well, that's where the one I saw came from. They come from the planet Skaro! What do they look like? An upside-down coffee cup with some of the little stirrer things stuck in it. Excellent. Never heard that one before. What's inside the armour? A gross alien mutant who thinks he's better than everyone else. What do the Daleks want? Same thing guys like that always want – to get rid of anyone who isn't like them. Why would you not want to be stuck in a room with one? Daleks have zero chill. They exterminate first, ask questions later.

THE DOCTOR'S GRADE: A

Excellent start – I always forget that not everyone knows as much about the Daleks as I do . . .

billpotts
Somewhere in Time

None
thedoctor #DALEKALLIES Davros: Created the Daleks. Not a nice person.

billpotts
Somewhere in Space

4 likes
thedoctor #DALEKENEMIES Movellans: Went to war with the Daleks and won.

Nardole's Codebreaker

Use the key on page 5 to decode this fact!

Pyramid Puzzle

THE MONKS HAVE HIDDEN FIFTEEN WORDS IN ONE OF THEIR PYRAMIDS. FIND THEM ALL BEFORE THE MONKS TAKE OVER THE EARTH!

YOU ARE EMPOWERED TO COMPLETE THIS CHALLENGE AS A REPRESENTATIVE OF HUMANITY.

- EXTREMIS
- VERITAS
- ANGELO
- POPE
- PYRAMID
- PRESIDENT
- GLOBAL
- MONK
- BRABBIT
- PLANTICOLA
- STATUE
- MEMORY
- BLOODLINE
- CATHEDRAL
- LYNCHPIN

```
            S T
          S U P M B C
          N P N L Z Z
          Q S R O C X
        Y Z T O O H N
        H Y A H D J M E
        P E T E L S B S
      S N A U C I T D Y G
      J Q A E F N J O S L
    D B P X O O E M A Q G H
    I K K G I Q Z T Y W N Z
    B I J Y P U O I I C Y G K N
    R A N A N O R A F Y J E S K
  Y A I T S V E P B L A Q K R Q N
  W B W G E V T F E X I N M Z G P
  V M B G V G V Y H P O A A G G P Z M
  T H I O M E M O R Y Y Q I N E K V Y
  T H M T T W R G R E O L R D B V L S K I
  T Z O N K Y S I Y L W A X A T G C O F H
  B L E K T I A N G G L O B A L M L T L X I I
  F L A G L Y C H A G V F D O U W I N Y R S P
  T T K T D E N P X F D H D G K O Y N D N S R B N
  B J X C A T H E D R A L B D O R Y B E C I M Y C
  X C X C G R R B C K C L I I P B N G E C H O B O Q S
  S M U M L R P L A N T I C O L A Y Y T T P U K F N V
  Q C P R E S I D E N T J O P R W F I M H Q I E J Z Y K Z
  H Z G Z P A E L D H H T E X T R E M I S N X N B X R I G S P
```

Trials of the TARDIS

Eaten!

When I got this face, the very first thing I had to do was remove the TARDIS – and myself – from the belly of a peckish T-Rex.

Transformed!

The Master stole my TARDIS and turned it into a Paradox Machine so he could mess with human history. The poor old girl was in a right state.

Shrunk!

After an energy drain, the outside of the TARDIS became so small that Clara could fit it in her handbag. I was inside, which was inconvenient.

POLICE PUBLIC CALL BOX

POLICE TELEPHONE
FREE
FOR USE OF
PUBLIC

ADVICE & ASSISTANCE
OBTAINABLE IMMEDIATELY
OFFICERS
RESPOND

PULL

You don't steer the TARDIS, you negotiate with it! The TARDIS tries to keep me out of danger, but it's quite good at getting into trouble too . . .

Rammed!

It was a bit of a shock when the hull of the *Titanic* came crashing through the TARDIS wall – especially because the TARDIS was flying across space at the time.

I SPEND MOST OF MY TIME IN THE CONTROL ROOM, BUT THE TARDIS ALSO HAS SOME FANTASTIC FACILITIES . . .

- **LIBRARY**
- **SWIMMING POOL**
- **ZERO ROOM**
- **ART GALLERY**
- **OBSERVATORY**
- **ZOO**
- **LABORATORY**
- **SICKBAY**
- **SQUASH COURT**
- **FOOD MACHINE**
- **MACAROON DISPENSER**

Sometimes I have to delete a few rooms, but I can always restore them later if I need to.

Bullseye!

Robin Hood rudely made a hole in the door with one of his arrows. No laughing matter. Luckily for him, the TARDIS repaired itself.

Obliterated!

The Daleks thought they'd destroyed the TARDIS, but didn't count on the Hostile Action Displacement System. It moves the ship away from danger – as long as I remember to turn it on!

BUILDING A TARDIS IN TWO EASY STEPS BY NARDOLE

First, you've got to imagine a very big box fitting inside a very small box. Then you've got to make one. It's the second part people get stuck on . . .

The Doctor asks . . .

What kind of TARDIS do I have?

A: Type 4

B: Type 40

C: Type 400

What's Your Time-Traveller

WHICH TARDIS TRAVELLER ARE YOU MOST LIKE? FOLLOW THE ARROWS TO FIND OUT!

START

Congratulations! You're on board the TARDIS. Where do you want to go first?

The future

The past

You see a dinosaur! What do you do?

Watch it from a distance

March up and say hello!

You arrive on a spaceship. What's the first thing you do?

Check the TARDIS readings for danger

Head straight out to explore

Are you good at following the rules?

Only if I agree with them!

Yes, I'm very conscientious and reliable

What would you say if you got the chance to go Mars?

I'd rather go somewhere I knew more about

Yes please! I want to see the whole universe

An alien creature appears in front of you! How do you react?

Wow! I wonder who this is?

Argh! Let's get back to the TARDIS!

YOU'RE MOST LIKE...
Bill

You're bright, brave and naturally curious about the world around you, but can sometimes be shy and awkward with new people. It's never long before you find your feet – after that, you give everything 110 per cent, and you're quick to spot important stuff that others don't notice.

YOU'RE MOST LIKE...
Nardole

You're not so confident in difficult situations, and prefer to know what you're up against before you go charging in. But you're very honest and reliable – if anyone ever wants to make sure a vault is safely guarded for 1000 years, you're just the person to make it happen!

Style?

Does being nosey often get you into trouble?

No, I prefer to mind my own business!

Sometimes, but I like to know what's going on!

Do you prefer to be the leader or are you happy to follow?

I just go with the flow

I'm in charge. Always.

Would you be happy to travel in someone else's TARDIS?

As long as it got me where I wanted to go

Certainly not! I need one of my own!

You land on a new planet. Do you care what the people there think of you?

Yes, I like to be liked – although I'm no pushover

No! They can like me or lump me!

Would you prefer a busy planet or a lonely moon?

A planet! I love being around other people

The moon! I like my own space

Are you ever rude to people without realising?

No, I'm very charming at all times!

Yes, but I always mean well

YOU'RE MOST LIKE . . .
Missy

Don't worry – that doesn't mean you're evil! You're just sharp, funny and super clever, and people find you exciting to be around – even when you're being bossy. Though you often prefer your own company, you also like to have the respect of people you admire, and love it when they say something nice.

YOU'RE MOST LIKE...
The Doctor

You're a very strong, independent character, and don't particularly care if people like you. Luckily that's not usually a problem, as most people you meet think you're amazing! You're never cruel or cowardly, and you never give up – the perfect qualities for a time-traveller.

The Tenth Planet

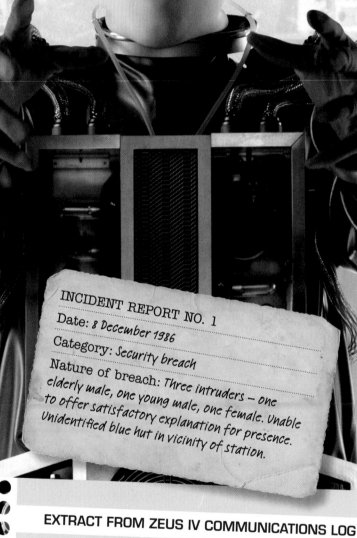

I'VE FOUGHT THE CYBERMEN ALL ACROSS TIME AND SPACE, BUT THE FIRST TIME I MET THEM THEY WERE MUCH CLOSER TO HOME . . .

MISSION: ZEUS IV LAUNCH

Snowcap space tracking station will monitor the launch of Zeus IV, the atmospheric testing probe.

PILOTS: Schultz and Williams

STATION COMMANDER: General Cutler

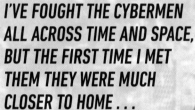

Polly and I were travelling with the Doctor. We'd not long met him, but we'd already seen things you wouldn't believe! Anyway, that day we ended up at the South Pole, Antarctica. There was a military base there, and they weren't pleased to see us . . .

INCIDENT REPORT NO. 1

Date: 8 December 1986

Category: Security breach

Nature of breach: Three intruders – one elderly male, one young male, one female. Unable to offer satisfactory explanation for presence. Unidentified blue hut in vicinity of station.

EXTRACT FROM ZEUS IV COMMUNICATIONS LOG

SCHULTZ: There's another planet out there!

WILLIAMS: Yeah, you're right. I can't see properly, but it reads as if it was in orbit between Mars and Venus.

SCHULTZ: Yeah, that's it. Funny how I can't put me finger on it, but it looks kind of familiar . . .

Mondas was originally the tenth planet orbiting the Sun. It drifted into deep space, but the Mondasians piloted the planet back to its original location, next to Earth. Mondasians were once like humans, but swapped their biological elements for mechanical parts and removed all emotions. They planned to drain Earth of energy and take humans to Mondas for Cyber-conversion.

INCIDENT REPORT NO. 2

Date: 8 December 1986

Category: Fatal security breach

Nature of breach: Alien space capsule has landed. Robotic creatures have taken over. They say they are from Earth's twin planet, Mondas. Designation: Cybermen. Activating panic button!

POSTAL TELEGRAPH COMMERCIAL CABLES
TELEGRAM

The Postal Telegraph-Cable Company (Incorporated) transmits and delivers this message subject to the terms and conditions printed on the back of this blank.

COUNTER NUMBER. | TIME FILED. | CHECK.

Send the following message, without repeating, subject to the terms and conditions printed on the back hereof, which are hereby agreed to.

URGENT MESSAGE FROM SNOWCAP STATION
From: General Cutler
To: Secretary General, International Space Command
SIR. REQUEST URGENT PERMISSION TO DETONATE
Z-BOMB AND NEUTRALISE CYBERMAN THREAT.
WILL CAUSE GRAVE LOSS OF LIFE ON EARTH. OUR
SITUATION IS DESPERATE.

Here I am – the original me, you might say – meeting the Mondasian Cybermen for the first time. Let's hope it's some time before we meet again . . .

Cutler had gone mad. He wanted to launch the Z-bomb – a series of nuclear bombs that would destroy Mondas, but with radiation fallout that would kill many humans too – so we got to work disarming it. We thought the Cybermen would kill us, but Mondas started to disintegrate. It couldn't take the strain of drawing power from Earth, and neither could the Cybermen. They all fell to bits.

This adventure took a great toll on the Doctor. He hadn't been well and was coming in and out of consciousness. We got him back to the TARDIS, and he started to glow, with a fierce, terrifying light. Everything was about to change forever . . .

Missy on Trial

MISSY, ALSO KNOWN AS THE MASTER, YOU ARE CHARGED WITH CRIMES AGAINST THE UNIVERSE THROUGHOUT ALL YOUR LIVES. IF YOU ARE FOUND GUILTY, THE SENTENCE IS DEATH. PREPARE TO DEFEND YOURSELF!

CASE 1
The Harold Saxon Incident

The charge: That you did unlawfully take control of Earth and decimate the population.

The defence: Decimate. I love that word. But I'm afraid you haven't got your facts right. Yes, I did become Prime Minister of the UK and enslave the population of Earth, then eliminated precisely one tenth of that population. But I think you'll find that the Doctor turned back time and undid all my bad work, so technically none of it ever happened. What have you got to say to THAT?

CASE 2
The 3W Institute Affair

The charge: That you did unlawfully kill Petronella Osgood as part of your plan to raise an army of Cybermen.

The defence: Well, you see, I really had no choice – she was a threat to me and my Cyberdears, so she had to go. But you can't find me guilty of that either – check the UNIT personnel files and you'll find not one but TWO Petronella Osgoods in active service. You can't convict me of killing someone who's still alive! Twice! Nice try, though.

CASE 3
The Devil's End Daemon

The charge: That you did impersonate a vicar then summon a cloven-hoofed daemon to take over the world.

The defence: How could I resist becoming a vicar, once the idea was in my head? All that dressing up and giving long speeches was right up my street! The taking-over-the-world bit was almost incidental. Anyway, I've already stood trial and gone to prison on Earth for this. Have you never heard of double jeopardy? You can't try someone twice for the same crime!

CASE 4
The Death Zone

The charge: That you did kidnap the Doctor, his previous selves, and beings from around the galaxy, then set them down to do battle in the Death Zone on Gallifrey.

The defence: Oh, not AGAIN! I'm always being accused of this, and for a change it wasn't my fault. The High Council of Time Lords told me that all the Doctors had disappeared and asked me to the Death Zone to look for them. I went, and what thanks did I get? None! I found the Doctors and they accused me of capturing them, when it was actually their pal President Borusa. Then the Brigadier punched me and I spent the rest of the day tied up on the floor! I'm not 'fessing up to this one.

CASE 5
The Bloodline Termination

The charge: That you did push a little girl into a volcano on the planet Riga-Priam.

The defence: Yes, I pushed her. And I'd do it again! Those annoying Monks were marching around Riga-Priam like they owned the place, stopping me from robbing the planet's quartz reserves. I had to break their control over the population, passed down through the bloodline to the brat. So, I just thought 'Into the lava with her!' and the link was broken! Perfectly reasonable. What? Why are you making that face?

MISSED ME!

Just how did I get out of these sticky situations?

1.
CHUCKED BACK INTO THE TIME WAR

I lurked in a pocket universe for a bit, then sneaked back out.

ZAPPED BY A CYBERMAN

Used the blast to recharge my Vortex Manipulator, then was off.

2.

3.
MAROONED ON SKARO

Not telling you how I got out of this one – but it was EVER so clever!

The Doctor asks...

What did Missy use to create her army of Cybermen?

A: Cyber Lightning

B: Cyber Pollen

C: Cyber Rain

WE WILL TAKE THIS PLANET AND ITS PEOPLE.

U.G.L.Y.

Withered, old skin

Human shape

Oi! We don't judge!

Claws like a skeleton

Dusty robes, like old curtains

Veritas

INFO DUMP

They're Monks, but not really Monks. So what are they? Aliens who want to conquer the Earth. Aren't they always? How did they plan to do it? They ran a simulation of all life on Earth so they knew how we'd react in every scenario. And then, invasion? No! These guys are too sly to do any invading. They wanted the human race to actually invite them to take over the planet. And they got me to do it, by asking for you to get your sight back, so you could save yourself from a deadly bacteria.
You gave away the world to save my life. I knew you would kick their butts if you could see again. And I was right. Took your time though. Six months to overthrow an invasion! That's pretty good. How did they take control? They were transmitting a signal to make everyone think they'd always been in charge. Created their own myth, and used me to spread it. So I used my memories to blank out theirs. I thought I wouldn't survive, but that didn't matter - as long as their lies died too.

billpotts
The Vault

billpotts
The Vault

1,971 likes
thedoctor #MONKENEMIES Missy - she had defeated them once before.

1,963 likes
thedoctor #MONKALLIES The Doctor, but he was only faking it.

THE DOCTOR'S GRADE: **A**
Very impressive, Bill - recalling details from false memories is a tricky business!

Nardole's Codebreaker

Use the key on page 5 to decode this fact!

[coded text symbols]

LOOSE IN THE LANE

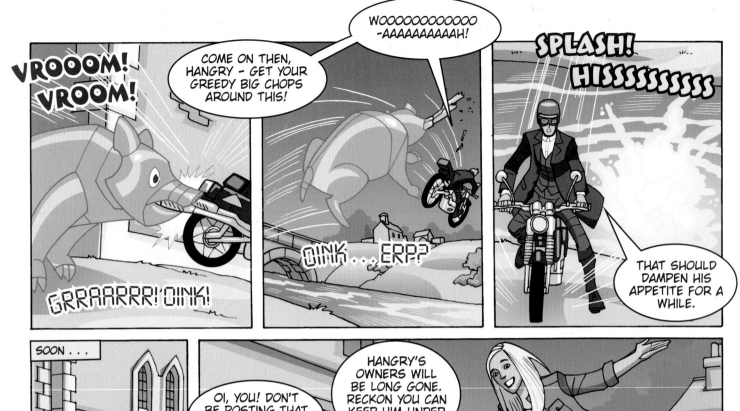

Walking on Thin Ice

THE ICE ON THE THAMES IS CRACKING! HELP THE ORPHANS LEAD FROST FAIR REVELLERS TO SAFETY, AVOIDING THE CRACKS AND THE CREATURE'S EYE.

The thaw is here! Quick, come with us!

It's a mistake, I tell you! The ice isn't melting!

START

END

Never underestimate the human ability to overlook the inexplicable!

Introducing...
Nardole

It's me, Nardy! You've met me before, but let's have a catch-up, shall we?

I'm Nardole, and I come from Mendorax Dellora, which is where I was first employed by Dr River Song. I helped her out on a job. A general admin job. Nothing criminal. Oh no. Definitely not.

I did enjoy working for River, even though I had my head cut off for my trouble. That experience made me rather suspicious of big, red robots for a long time . . .

Eventually, the Doctor put me back to how I was. Almost. My body's still a bit robotic, but at least it fits me now. I do tend to rattle and squeak, and sometimes the odd screw falls off and rolls under the sofa, but other than that I'm very happy.

When Dr Song died, she left strict instructions for me to look after the Doctor. I've done my best, but he's not easy to keep an eye on. I'd need more than two eyes for that. If I ever change my head again, I'll definitely think about adding a couple at the back.

I might not be human, but I've grown to love a lot of your strange habits and customs. I like tea – although I usually add a bit of coffee or it doesn't taste of much. I'm also a big fan of knitting. I make all my own hats!

I'm scared of heights, depths, small spaces, wide-open spaces, sharp instruments, blunt instruments . . . I'd rather have a quiet night in with a bowl of popcorn and a box set than be out there fighting Daleks. But don't underestimate me. I've got a Brown Tabard in Tarovian Martial Arts, and I'm not afraid to give your neck a good pinch if necessary!

For a while, my main job was making sure the Doctor stayed on Earth to guard the Vault, but he was constantly trying to give me the slip and go off into space. Sometimes I got bored of arguing and went along for the ride. I know it's naughty, but he's very persuasive . . .

I've been with the Doctor for a long time and I know about ten per cent of his secrets. I can also pilot the TARDIS. It sometimes takes me a few tries to get where I want to go – although I'd never have been Emperor of Constantinople otherwise, so it's not all bad.

ME AND DOCTOR MYSTERIO

The Doctor and I were investigating Harmony Shoal when we ran into an old friend of his – Grant Gordon, aka The Ghost. The Doctor had accidentally given him superpowers when he was young.

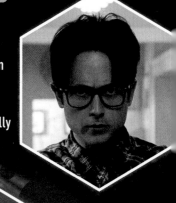

A load of alien brains were plotting to get themselves put into Earth leaders so they could take over . . .

Grant managed to stop the aliens from blowing up New York with their spaceship, right in the nick of time.

The Doctor was still very sad about River but he was back in business at last!

The Doctor asks . . .

On which planet did I find Nardole's head?

A: Gallifrey

B: Earth

C: Darillium

Life on Mars

CAN YOU MAKE YOUR WAY THROUGH THE TUNNELS UNDER THE SURFACE OF MARS AND GET TO EMPRESS IRAXXA'S HIVE BEFORE ANYONE ELSE?

A GAME FOR TWO OR MORE PLAYERS

YOU WILL NEED:
A dice and counters

26

25
You find the TARDIS. TRAVEL FORWARD TO 34.

24

23

START

1

27

44
Ice Warrior attack! GO BACK TO THE SPACE YOU CAME FROM.

43

2
Ice Warrior attack! GO BACK TO THE SPACE YOU CAME FROM.

28

45
You've run out of supplies. GO BACK 10 SPACES.

49
The door to the hive is locked. ROLL A 6 TO OPEN IT.

3
Rockfall. MISS A TURN.

29
Ice Warrior attack! GO BACK TO THE SPACE YOU CAME FROM.

46

47

48
Rockfall. MISS A TURN.

4

30

31
Ice Warrior attack! GO BACK TO THE SPACE YOU CAME FROM.

32

33

5
Catchlove claims Mars in the name of Queen Victoria. ROLL AGAIN.

6

7
Jackdaw starts singing. GO FORWARD 3 SPACES SO YOU CAN'T HEAR HIM.

8

9
DRILL THROUGH TO 33.

IRAXXA
Empress of Mars

FRIDAY
An Ice Warrior

COLONEL GODSACRE
A soldier

JACKDAW
A thief

CAPTAIN CATCHLOVE
A bounder!

22 DRILL THROUGH TO 42.

21

20 Ice Warrior attack! GO BACK TO THE SPACE YOU CAME FROM.

19

42

41

40 Rockfall. MISS A TURN.

39

18 You fall through the rock floor. GO BACK 4 SPACES.

50 You've reached the hive and made contact with the Federation delegate. *YOU ARE VICTORIOUS!*

38

17

37 You accidentally send yourself back to Earth in the TARDIS. GAME OVER!

16 Ice Warrior attack! GO BACK TO THE SPACE YOU CAME FROM.

34

35

36 DRILL THROUGH TO 12.

15

10

11 Friday's exhausted! MISS TWO TURNS WHILE HE HAS A REST.

12

13 Rockfall. MISS A TURN.

14

Our house fell down. Great!
So now we need to find a new one, fast.
What do you think of these?

and weekend hours available. Fax
application Attn: HR Dept.

Apply Today!

FULLY EQUIPPED MEDICAL BAY

- Hospital-style room with extensive life-support system
- Dalek attendants available 24/7
- Stunning views of the sunrise over Skaro's mountains
- Available immediately – previous occupant unexpectedly resumed plans to conquer the universe

Rent: 5.007 zegs per 700 rels

Apply to Mr D. Avros

EXCLUSIVE SUBTERRANEAN HIDEOUT

Leave the hustle and bustle behind for the peace and quiet of Roman Britain!

- Narrowly proportioned passageway hewn from the rock itself
- Aberdeen only two days away on horseback
- Fully lit by oil lamp
- Some noise from crows in the early morning
- No pets – especially not Pictish Beasts

Rent: 1 gold coin

Apply to Kar

ROOMS AVAILABLE IN ARISTOCRATIC RESIDENCE

Family home of Lord Sutcliffe, now affordable housing for the community. Priority will be given to orphans and other urchins. Great views of the Thames and exquisitely decorated. Free grub three times a day – help yourself!

Rent: Nominal
Apply to Kitty,
Lord Peregrine Sutcliffe's private secretary
TOFFS NEED NOT APPLY

SERIES TWELVE SMARTSUITS FOR HIRE

- Fully automated with on-board life support
- Built-in entertainment system
- OXYGEN NOT INCLUDED

Rent: Variable, according to market demand
Apply to Ganymede Systems

Classified Ads

COSY ROOM IN FAMILY HOME

- Fully furnished with bed, dressing table and mirror

- Landlady is like a mother to her tenants

- No time-wasters – last girl kept moving in and out!

Rent: Reasonable
Apply to Moira

Oi! That's my room!

INFO DUMP

Now, this whole business proves why you should ALWAYS pay attention in my lectures. Totally. I thought all that stuff about lungs exploding was weird when you said it, but it really came in handy. So, how did a load of series twelve smartsuits end up killing their occupants? It was all about the oxygen. The mining station (Chasm Forge) had none, except for what was in the suits. When the suits malfunctioned, the people died but the suits kept on going. Creepy.

The suits hadn't really malfunctioned, had they? Nope. All the suits got an order to cut off the oxygen supply at the same time. You thought it was a hacker, but the truth was much worse.

We'll get to that. What were the suits capable of? They were slow and clumsy inside, but really fast in space. And they started working stuff out, learning to solve problems! Mine turned against me and you had to give me your helmet. I did. And the suits needed to believe that you were dead for my plan to work... Yeah, thanks for that. I think I should get top marks just for being almost dead, actually.

Nice try, but no. Anyway, how was the situation resolved? You realised that Ganymede Systems were behind it all, killing off their miners because the station had become unprofitable. You threatened to blow it up, which would have cost them serious money, so instead we were all saved. Smart! Why thank you, Miss Potts.

YOUR LIFE IS IN OUR HANDS...

Forcefield to keep air in

Organic component

Otherwise known as a person!

This is its 'eye'

Good for gathering data

Rigid exoskeleton – it only moves when it wants to

billpotts
Chasm Forge

❤ 2,017 likes

thedoctor #SUITENEMIES Abby and Ivan, the last survivors on Chasm Forge.

...tor #SUITALLIES The bosses of Ganymede Systems.

Nardole's Codebreaker

Use the key on page 5 to decode this fact!

THE DOCTOR'S GRADE: A

A perfect study in what happens when profit overrules basic humanity. And I was left blind, which would soon prove rather inconveni...

MONDASIAN MYSTERY

THERE ARE TEN DIFFERENCES BETWEEN THESE TWO PICTURES OF THE DOCTOR AND FOUR SINISTER CYBERMEN. CAN YOU SPOT THEM ALL?

I AM THE DOCTOR

A flustered-looking figure in a red waistcoat was crashing around the Doctor's office, angrily shuffling papers and rattling teacups.

"This just won't do," he muttered to himself. "He made an oath. 'I won't go to space,' he says. And where is he?"

Nardole looked accusingly at the 'Out Of Order' sign lying on the floor where the TARDIS had been.

"Space!" he yelled. "Blinking, flipping Spacey McSpaceface! Honestly, he might be 2000 years old, but he's not too old for the naughty step . . ."

Just then, his rant was interrupted by a sharp knock at the door.

"Better not be students," Nardole seethed. "I'm in no mood for undergraduates today."

Noticing the Doctor's sonic sunglasses sitting on his desk, Nardole had a flash of inspiration.

I'll have a look with these, he thought.

He popped the glasses on and tapped the side, bringing up a wireframe view of the room. Beyond the door, Nardole could see the outline of whoever – or *whatever* – was outside.

"Hmm. There seem to be quite a lot of you,"

said Nardole. "I hope this isn't a prank. I don't care for pranks. Unless I'm doing the pranking."

He squinted and the sonic display came into focus, showing his unwelcome callers in greater detail. There were six of them – all very tall and wearing studded armour. And were those . . . *tusks*?

"Unlikely that they've just got lost on their way to a heavy-metal night at the student union, then," Nardole muttered.

The knock came again – more forcefully this time, causing the door to shudder.

"Show yourself, Doctor!" screeched an angry, shrill voice from the other side. "We have hunted you down to your coward's hiding hole! Now come out and face us, you wretched time weasel!"

Nardole backed up against the wall, trying hard not to panic. Whoever was outside didn't sound friendly, and the Doctor might be gone for days! What would happen if these creatures got their hands on the Vault?

"Erm, who's calling please?" he asked.

"I am Ratatoskr, leader of the 47th Marauding Horde of Ongatatis 5!" the stranger shrieked. "And I challenge you to a test of endurance against my chosen champion. The victor will be deemed master of this miserable space rock!"

Nardole dashed around, looking for something to defend himself with.

"Erm, can you come back at 6 o'clock please?" he said. "I'm, erm . . . I'm watching *The Chase*!"

Suddenly, Nardole spotted an old chest in the corner of the room. He rushed over to it and looked inside, a grin breaking out across his face.

"Oh, thank you, sir," he gasped. "I knew you wouldn't leave me defenceless!"

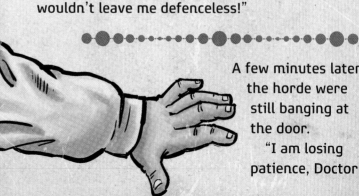

A few minutes later, the horde were still banging at the door.

"I am losing patience, Doctor!"

screeched Ratatoskr. "Show yourself immediately, or I will order my soldiers to devour the pathetic beasts of this wretched world, one by one!"

Then the door started to slowly creak open.

"Oh, you've just made a *big* mistake!" said Nardole from the other side, his voice deep and booming. "Because if you know who I am, you'll know that I won't let any harm come to this planet or the people on it!"

Nardole heard the floorboards creak as the horde took a step back.

"I am the Oncoming Storm, the mighty warrior, the destroyer of worlds, the drinker of tea and the . . . erm . . . eater of chips!"

The door burst fully open and there stood Nardole, wearing stripy brown trousers, a velvet jacket, a long multicoloured scarf, a red bow tie round his neck, and a floppy hat on top of his head.

"I AM THE DOCTOR!" he yelled. "AND YOU –" Nardole finally looked the 47th Marauding Horde of Ongatatis 5 up and down, and his face crumpled in surprise, "– are a gang of furry space squirrels!"

Ratatoskr and his gang were thin, gangly creatures with long tusks. Each member of the gang was puffing out their chest in an attempt to fill their ill-fitting metal armour, from the backs of which protruded an array of rather ratty tails.

Apparently trying to look as threatening as possible, Ratatoskr was frowning fiercely.

"Seriously?" Nardole chuckled. "You guys looked really scary on X-ray vision! Have you thought about becoming X-rays full time?"

"You insult us, Doctor!" Ratatoskr squawked. "And anyway, you don't look much like the Bringer of Darkness of which the legends speak."

Nardole was offended. "Well, let's just say we're both a bit disappointed," he said grumpily. "Now, I believe you said something about an endurance test?" He pointed down the corridor. "Shall we take this outside, Ratatouille?"

"*Ratatoskr*," snarled the squirrel creature.

"What*ever*," replied Nardole, creaking a little as he marched forward, leading the horde towards the university courtyard and hoping they wouldn't pass any students on the way.

Nardole shook as he stood outside, facing the Marauding Horde. Even though they weren't as scary as he'd first thought, Nardole had never been the Doctor before, and it wasn't quite as easy as Sir made it look.

He took a deep breath and flipped his stripy scarf dramatically round his neck.

"Now," he said. "As I am the registered protector of this world, I invoke Article 2367 of the Shadow Proclamation, giving me the right to set the rules of this challenge."

Ratatoskr gave a nasty grin, his arms folded. "Fine, because it doesn't matter what rules you set. You are no match for my champion."

The horde parted to reveal a member Nardole hadn't noticed before – a massive, hulking beast of a squirrel creature! His tusks were razor sharp and he had a tail so thick it made leaves fall from the tree branches above as he swished it.

"Meet my brother, Rataberserkr!" said Ratatoskr smugly. "Present your own champion, Doctor, or prepare to be vanquished!"

Nardole gulped. A fight against Rataberserkr wasn't going to go in his favour, and he didn't have anyone to offer up as champion. He needed to think of a plan. What would the Doctor do?

"WOOOOAAAAH!"

A sudden yell came from behind Nardole, and he jumped aside as a shopping trolley careered past him and crashed, tipping out the occupant.

A scrawny young man was now lying at his feet. Nardole bent down to help him, ignoring the impatient stares of the Marauding Horde.

"Another prank?" hissed Nardole. "Honestly, this university would run far smoother without any of you being here!" He looked at the boy closely. "Hold on, I know you! You're Bill's friend Harry."

Harry grinned back at him. "That's right," he replied. "And you're the Doctor's . . . what are you, again? His butler? His PA?"

Nardole shook his head violently. "I need help!" he whispered. "Please, go along with what I say."

Harry got to his feet and nodded. "No problem, fella, anything you – WOAH!" he cried, now face-to-face with the horde. "Great costumes! Are you boys from the Cosplay Society?"

Nardole nodded enthusiastically. "Yes, that's right. And I'm cosplaying the Doctor!"

Before Harry he could ask any more questions, Nardole grabbed his hand and stuck it into the air.

"Here he is!" he announced. "Just in time. Earth's mighty main man, Harry!"

Ratatoskr walked round Harry, inspecting him. "This *child*?" he scoffed. "This half-man is your planet's champion?"

Nardole looked serious. "Yes," he said in a grave voice, adjusting his bow tie with confidence. "Now, everyone, follow me."

●●●●●●· · · ●●●●· · · ●●●●●

The unlikely group assembled at the base of two matching statues in front of one of the university's oldest buildings. Nardole carefully placed a traffic cone alongside each, explaining the rules of his challenge as he did so.

"What I ask of you may sound simple enough. But this is the ultimate Earth test of prowess, agility and balance, devised by the brightest minds at this university," he boomed. "Only the most able are fit to complete it. Are you *sure* you are willing to take on the challenge?"

Ratatoskr scowled. "This is a juvenile's provocation – an insult to the great warrior Rataberserkr!" he screeched. "But it is one at

which he will easily triumph. We accept!"

Nardole looked at Harry. "And what of you, young sir? Are you willing and able?"

Harry bounced up and down on the spot. "You bet! I've been training for this one for years!"

Harry and Rataberserkr took their places beside their respective traffic cones.

"On your marks, get set . . . GO!" cried Nardole.

The two contenders threw their cones up on to the plinths and clambered after them. They swiftly started shinning up the statues – Harry's cone tucked under his arm, Rataberserkr's clamped in his large teeth. Rataberserkr's physical fitness was matched by Harry's wiry, nimble moves, and the two were neck and neck all the way up.

"Victory!" Rataberserkr shouted, as he tossed his traffic cone on to the statue's head a second before Harry jammed his on.

The Marauding Horde crowed in delight as the two champions climbed back down.

"Glory to Ongatatis 5!" screeched the scrawny squirrel. "So much for your champion, Doctor. We will now take control of this planet, and there's nothing you can do about it!"

Nardole pointed up to Rataberserkr's statue. "I wouldn't be so sure about that," he said. "The terms of the Great Cone on a Statue Challenge were very clear. The cone must remain firmly on the statue's head for five minutes, otherwise the contender is disqualified!"

As he spoke, Rataberserkr's cone wobbled and fell off the statue, landing on his head.

"What an amateur!" said Harry, looking up to admire his own cone, which was still firmly in position on top of the statue. "If you want a traffic cone put on top of a statue, just ask a student. We're the experts!"

Ratatoskr squared up to Nardole, tail bristling.

"You have tricked us, Doctor," he fumed. "Your mental agility is as deadly as the legends say after all! But we have honour as warriors, even if you have none. So we will leave you and your pathetic world as promised."

Ratatoskr started to march off, his dejected horde trotting behind him. "We didn't even want to conquer it, so THERE!"

Later, over a pot of tea in the Doctor's office, Nardole and Harry told the real Time Lord and Bill about their heroic victory.

"And there were at least fifty of them, weren't there, Harry?" gasped Nardole.

"Oh, at least!" agreed Harry. "Massive, they were. All about three metres tall."

"Is that so?" asked the Doctor. "Well, they must have been working out on Ongatatis 5 since I was last there," he said, raising an eyebrow.

Harry frowned. "What's Ongatatis 5? I thought they were cosplayers?"

"I'll explain it to you later," Bill laughed.

Nardole stood up and started clearing away the teacups. "Back to work for me, then," he sighed. "Shame. I enjoyed being the Doctor for the day."

The Doctor looked at him. "Just one thing that doesn't make sense, Nardole," he said. "There's no such thing as Article 2367 of the Shadow Proclamation. It only goes up to Article 2366."

Nardole tried his best to look innocent. "Really, sir?" he said. "That's awful. Imagine if the 47th Marauding Horde of Ongatatis 5 had noticed that. Why, they might not have let me choose that ridiculous challenge, and everyone on Earth would've been nibbled to death by big squirrels!"

And, with that, Nardole shuffled away, teacups in hand and the corner of a bright-red bow tie just peeking out of his pocket.

Postcards From the Universe

THE DOCTOR'S FRIENDS HAVE BEEN SENDING POSTCARDS ABOUT THEIR LATEST ADVENTURES. WHY NOT SEND THEM ONE BACK FROM EARTH?

Greetings from MARS

May it please Your Majesty,

I wish to inform you that I have led a successful mission to the planet Mars.

We hoped to claim the Red Planet in the name of Queen Victoria, but when we arrived it transpired they already had a marvellous queen of their own. (Well, more of an empress, really.)

Alas, Captain Catchlove was killed in action. With no way back to Earth, I have pledged allegiance to Empress Iraxxa and will serve her in your honour. I have requested that the traveller known as the Doctor deliver this card to you personally, so I trust it will reach you safely.

I have the honour to remain, madam, Your Majesty's most humble and obedient servant.

Your truly,
Colonel Godsacre

POST

Dear Velma,

I know it's been a while, but I heard something recently that made me think of you and all the old memories came flooding back (eventually).

How's work? Still doing the acting? You do have a lovely voice. I'm travelling at the moment – have just visited a space station and met some smashing people. Quite a few of them did end up turning into space zombies, though, which was a bit of a shame.

Maybe we can meet for fizzy pop and crisps next time you're near the Milky Way? I'll send you a picture of my latest head, so you know who to look for.

Love,
Your dearest Nardole

Visit Chasm Forge!

POST CARD

PRINTED IN ENGLAND

FOR CORRESPONDENCE | FOR ADDRESS ONLY

Dear Doctor,

Did you forget something when you did a runner from Davros's lab? OH YES, THAT'S RIGHT - ME!

Well, luckily for you, I'm having a brilliant time here on Skaro. I'm just back from a dip in the Ocean of Ooze, and I might take a stroll through the Petrified Forest after lunch to pick myself a nice bunch of Varga Plants - as long as the

radiation readings aren't too high. I've even got myself a pet Slyther. I've named him 'Doctor'! He's very well behaved, but does tend to eat any Thals we meet, so I'm not very popular with them.

Looking forward to spending a LOT of time with you soon . . . Toodles!

Missy x

GUARANTEED REAL PHOTOGRAPH

Skaro

It's so bracing!

SMILE
You're on Gliese 581 D!

Hi Moira,

Don't know if this will get to you - the stamps here have got emojis on them instead of the Queen - but I posted it anyway.

So, you know how you're always saying I'll never go anywhere in life? Well, guess what? I've gone to another planet! This card is coming direct from an Earth colony, in the future, with two suns! Amazing wildlife too. Well, the Vardy are friendly, as long as you keep smiling . . .

Bill :)

P.S. Don't rent my room out to anyone while I'm gone!

Moira Po

Flat 6

The Hei

Brist

Write your message here!

PostCard

Come to Earth and visit

The Cathedral!

It's always been here!

FROM:

43

Bill's Assignment: Emojibots

THE DOCTOR'S GRADE: A

Perfect comprehension of a tricky topic. But what is it with you and things that move like penguins?

INFO DUMP

They're called Emojibots, but are they proper robots? No, just an interface. The Vardy are the real robots – the Emojibots just let humans communicate with the Vardy. What are they communicating about?

The Vardy are worker robots for the humans colonising Gliese 851 D. Whole flocks of them, building and working together to keep the human settlers happy all the time.

And how do they know if the humans are happy? Everyone gets a badge on their back, showing an emoji that reflects their feelings. There's one big problem with this system – do you know what it is? Nobody can be happy all the time! The first time someone died on Gliese 851 D, the Emojibots told the Vardy to kill everyone who was sad and grieving. The Emojibots didn't understand that grief was natural and unavoidable.

And then a very clever person did a clever thing to stop all the colonists who were still in deep-freeze from being killed too. You mean you turned the Emojibots off and on again to reset them? I mean I turned them off and on again, yes. Well, it worked! Without the Emojibots to tell the Vardy what to do, they forgot who the humans even were and started all over again with a clean slate.

Eyes change to show mood

Digital display for a face

If they hug you, you're in trouble

Quick sonic here to reset

Super-tight grip

Short legs make them waddle like a penguin

ENEMIES
Humans. Too emo for them to deal with.

ALLIES
The Vardy – flocks of tiny worker robots.

Nardole's Codebreaker

Use the key on page 5 to decode this fact!

MISSY LOVES GHOSTIE

THERE SHE IS!

NOOOOOOOO!

THE AMULET LANDS ON MISSY!

OH, GHOSTIE-WHOSTIE! IS IT TOO LATE TO CHANGE MY MIND?

I'D LOVE TO MARRY YOU!

GRAB HER!

DO YOU MIND? I'M TRYING TO GET ENGAGED HERE!

AAAAARGH!

WOAH! YOU DIDN'T HAVE TO DO THAT.

NOW, WHERE WERE WE? AH YES. I WILL MARRY YOU.

WELL, I CAN'T. I'M ALREADY GETTING MARRIED.

TO LUCY. AND I LOVE HER, NOT YOU.

HOW SWEET! I MARRIED A LUCY ONCE, TOO.

BUT NOW I'LL HAVE TO KILL EVERY SINGLE LUCY IN NEW YORK. JUST TO BE SURE.

NO! WAIT! PLEASE!

AND I'D BETTER KILL EVERYONE ELSE, TOO. JUST TO BE REALLY SURE!

I CAN USE THIS THING TO BOOST THE RANGE . . .

MISSY, NO! IF YOU REALLY LOVE ME, YOU WON'T DO THIS. PLEASE!

THE END

INFO DUMP

Today's subject: inhabitants of Mars.

The Nice Warriors!

Very amusing. What do you know about the species?

They look pretty scary, but they're actually a noble and intelligent race. Yeah, they're aggressive when it comes to war and that, but really they're just as civilised as humans. Some would say more civilised, at times. Their civilisation is very complex.   I get you. Love a bit of war, but into beautiful stuff as well.

When we turned up, most of them were hibernating. They were - until the nineteenth-century English blokes who'd ended up on Mars started drilling through to the hive. Those guys thought they were going to run around the planet like they owned it, but that's not how it worked out. Just like on Earth. Their plan didn't work though, did it?   They woke up the Empress Iraxxa, and she was not happy to have her hibernation interrupted. As far as she was concerned, it was an invasion.

I warned the Empress that the surface of Mars was uninhabitable...   Yeah, mansplaining her own planet to her! Once we'd talked it out, woman to woman, she was a lot cooler. She called off her Warriors and admitted she needed help.

The mouth is its weakest point

Eye-protection visors

One of Friday's was damaged

Bio-mechanical armour

The true creature is inside

Sonic weapon

THE DOCTOR'S GRADE: A

I knew I'd make a diplomat out of you one day. Maybe you could get a job with the Galactic Federation when you graduate?

billpotts
Mars

♡ 1,967 likes
thedoctor #ICEWARRIORALLIES Iraxxa, the mighty Empress of Mars.

billpotts
Mars

♡ 1,881 likes
thedoctor #ICEWARRIORENEMIES Catchlove, a greedy and selfish human.

Nardole's Codebreaker

Use the key on page 5 to decode this fact!

GETTING EMOJI-NAL

> Remember to keep smiling while you complete these three mega challenges!

CAN YOU DECIPHER WHICH FIVE OF THE DOCTOR'S ADVENTURES HAVE BEEN SCRAMBLED HERE?

NGYXOE

CKKON NKCKO

ETH NERUTR FO RCDOTO ISEORYTM

HNIT EIC

HET OILTP

ONLY TWO OF THESE EMOJIBOTS ARE IDENTICAL. HOW QUICKLY CAN YOU SPOT THE MATCHING PAIR?

TAKE THE FIRST LETTER OF YOUR NAME

A Best	N Super
B Star	O Majestic
C Sun	P Royal
D Misty	Q Soar
E Brave	R Awesome
F Clever	S Perfect
G Calm	T Fine
H Prime	U Calm
I Gentle	V Humble
J Happy	W Bright
K Strong	X Tough
L Friend	Y Fly
M High	Z Amazing

NOW TAKE THE MONTH YOU WERE BORN IN

January:	mist
February	fast
March:	moon
April:	day
May:	gaze
June:	break
July:	worthy
August:	time
September:	feeling
October:	shine
November:	flight
December:	thing

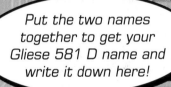

Put the two names together to get your Gliese 581 D name and write it down here!

I'm Goodthing.

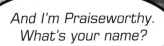

And I'm Praiseworthy. What's your name?

53

The Twelfth Doctor's
Best Bits

I've had some great times while I've had this face. Here are some of my special favourites . . .

Best THREAT!

Can you hurry up please, or I'll hit you with my shoe!

Best DANCE!

What? If you'd just managed to save your tiny, miniaturised self from being squashed by a train, you'd feel like doing a little dance too.

Best ENTRANCE!

Looking back, I didn't do a particularly good job of trying to hide out in the Middle Ages without attracting attention . . .

Best FIGHT!

I am the Doctor, and this is my spoon!

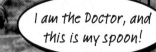

Best TRIUMPH!

It took me more than four billion years, but, just like the little bird with its sharp beak, I eventually punched my way through a solid Azbantium wall.

Best TARDIS TOUR!

It looks like . . .

A spaceship!

. . . a kitchen!

I always love showing off my magnificent control room for the first time – but nobody has ever reacted quite like Bill.

STUPENDOUS SPEECHES

I CAN MAKE AN ENTIRE ARMY TURN AND RUN WITH JUST WORDS . . .

"Human progress isn't measured by industry. It's measured by the value you place on a life. An unimportant life. A life without privilege. The boy who died on the river, that boy's value is your value. That's what defines an age. That's what defines a species."

"You don't have to be real to be the Doctor. Long as you never give up. Long as you always trick the bad guys into their own traps."

"And do you know what you do with all that pain? You hold it tight. And you say this: no one else will ever have to live like this. No one else will ever have to feel this pain. Not on my watch."

Best SURPRISE!

Hello, sweetie.

River Song didn't recognise me with my latest face. Hers was a picture when the penny finally dropped.

Best CUPPA!

The real question, of course, is where did I get the cup of tea? Answer: I'm the Doctor; just accept it.

Best PUNCH!

I just wanted to know how long it takes before you can make a speech like the one you just made. It was worth the wait.

Best SLEIGH RIDE!

It's not every day that Santa himself gives you a shot at riding in his sleigh. Rudolph doesn't usually like strangers, for a start

IN THE SHADOWS

CAN YOU HELP THE DOCTOR IDENTIFY THE CREATURES HE'S SPOTTED THROUGH HIS SONIC SUNGLASSES?

My enemies can't know I've been blind since Chasm Forge . . . you have to help me!

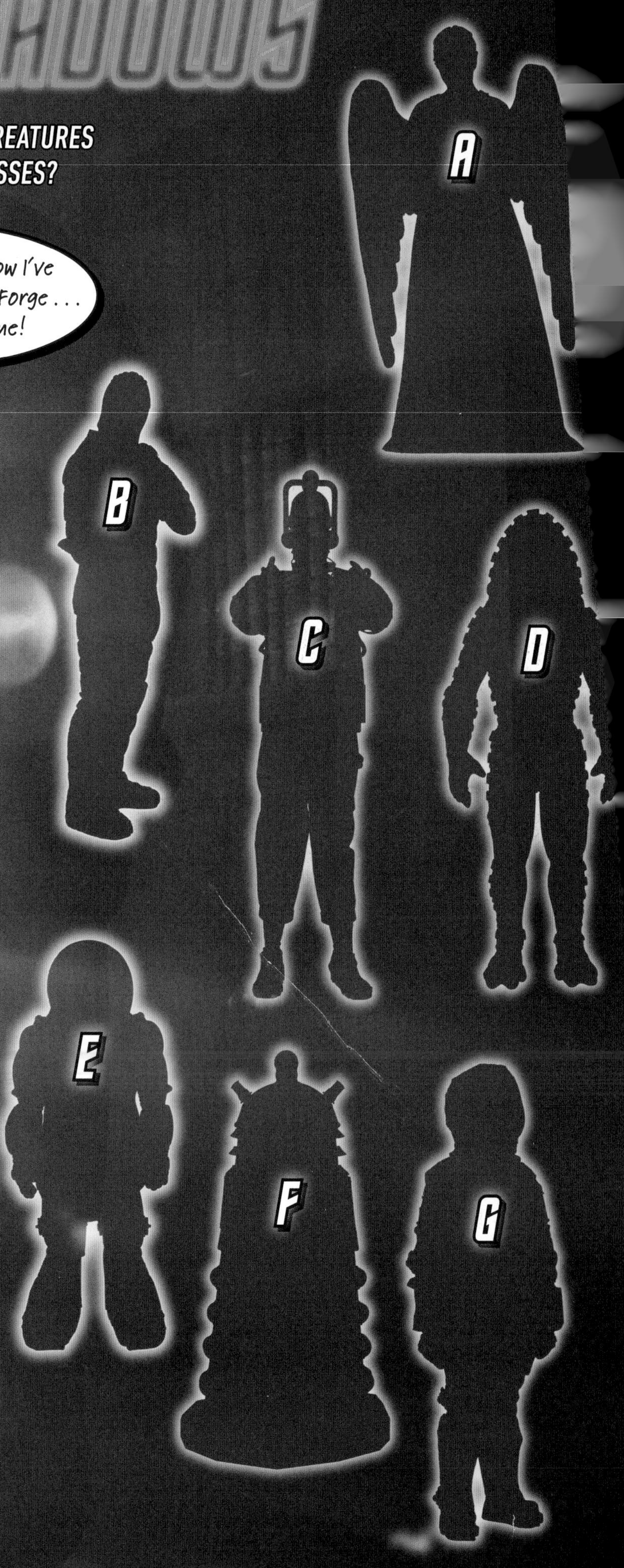

A

B

C

D

E

F

G

Cyberman

Suit

Emojibot

Ice Warrior

Dalek

Zygon

Weeping Angel

NO.
DAT

Turned totally into wood!

Mind you don't get a splinter . . .

The lice gathered energy to keep her alive

Lice crawling under her skin! Yuck!

Human sacrifices needed to restore her every twenty years

ALLIES
The lice, used by the Landlord to restore his sick mother.

ENEMIES
ME! These guys really ruined my day.

Nardole's Codebreaker

Use the key on page 5 to decode this fact!

INFO DUMP

Now, this escapade proves that it's not always scary-looking monsters you have to watch out for. Definitely not. This was a whole load of trouble, caused mainly by one human.
It also proves that if an offer seems too good to be true it probably is. All right, no need to rub it in. My mates and I were desperate when the Landlord offered us somewhere to live, so we snapped it up.
I won't say I told you so, but it did all go very wrong, very quickly. I know. We didn't even have anywhere to plug our phones in.
I was referring to all your friends going missing . . .
Oh yeah, that. The Landlord was really creepy, hanging around the house all the time . . . Turned out he was summoning these weird alien woodlice and they were eating my mates! Presumably they weren't just hungry? No. He had a woman named Eliza hidden in the tower. She'd become ill many years ago and the Landlord had discovered that the lice could restore her, so he'd kept her alive by sacrificing others.

Eliza thought the Landlord was her father, when he was actually her son. Yup. And, when she realised, she didn't want to go on living that lonely life in the tower. She sacrificed herself - and him - then got the lice to bring back my friends. And then our house fell down. Brilliant.

THE DOCTOR'S GRADE: A

A good lesson in how things are not always as they first appear. And also in not renting the first house you find.

THE FINAL EXAM

I'VE HAD LOTS OF ADVENTURES – AND I
REMEMBER EVERY SINGLE ONE. BUT DO YOU?

Can you match each picture to the right adventure? Tick all the ones you've seen!

Write the correct number here!

Deep Breath

Into the Dalek

Robot of Sherwood

Listen

Time Heist

The Caretaker

Kill the Moon

Mummy on the Orient Express

Flatline

In the Forest of the Night

Dark Water

Death in Heaven

Last Christmas

The Magician's Apprentice

The Witch's Familiar

Under the Lake

Before the Flood

The Girl Who Died

The Woman Who Lived

The Zygon Invasion

The Zygon Inversion

Sleep No More

Face the Raven

Heaven Sent

Hell Bent

The Husbands of River Song

The Return of Doctor Mysterio

The Pilot

Smile

Thin Ice

Knock Knock

Oxygen

Extremis

The Pyramid at the End of the World

The Lie of the Land

Empress of Mars

The Eaters of Light

World Enough and Time

The Doctor Falls

Answers

P.10–11 Introducing . . . Bill Potts
A: A kitchen

P.12 Bill's Assignment: The Daleks
THE MOVELLANS CREATED A VIRUS THAT WAS DEADLY TO DALEKS.

P.13 Pyramid Puzzle

P.14–15 Trials of the TARDIS
B: Type 40

P.20–21 Missy on Trial
B: Cyber Pollen

P.22 Bill's Assignment: The Monks
THE MONKS CHOOSE A PSYCHIC LINK CALLED 'THE LYNCHPIN'.

P.30–31 Introducing . . . Nardole
C: Darillium

P.36 Bill's Assignment: The Suits
THE SCAREDER YOU ARE, THE MORE OXYGEN YOU USE.

P.29 Walking on Thin Ice

P.37 Mondasian Mystery

P.44 Bill's Assignment: Emojibots
THE SETTLEMENT CITY WAS NAMED EREHWON.

P.51 Bill's Assignment: Ice Warriors
ICE WARRIORS ARE REPTILIAN WITH STRONG CLAWS.

P.52–53 Getting Emoji-nal
Oxygen, Knock Knock, The Return of Doctor Mysterio, Thin Ice, The Pilot
C and E are identical

P.56 In the Shadows
C: Cyberman, G: Suit, E: Emojibot,
B: Ice Warrior, F: Dalek, D: Zygon,
A: Weeping Angel

P.57 Bill's Assignment: The Landlord and Eliza
THE LANDLORD'S NAME WAS JOHN.

P.58–59 The Final Exam
11 – Deep Breath, 39 – Into the Dalek, 30 – Robot of Sherwood, 14 – Listen, 34 – Time Heist, 32 – The Caretaker, 23 – Kill the Moon, 16 – Mummy on the Orient Express, 6 – Flatline , 2 – In the Forest of the Night, 13 – Dark Water, 7 – Death in Heaven, 24 – Last Christmas, 35 – The Magician's Apprentice, 4 – The Witch's Familiar, 21 – Under the Lake, 22 – Before the Flood, 25 – The Girl Who Died, 18 – The Woman Who Lived, 15 – The Zygon Invasion, 37 – The Zygon Inversion, 9 – Sleep No More, 8 – Face the Raven, 26 – Heaven Sent, 28 – Hell Bent, 38 – The Husbands of River Song, 20 – The Return of Doctor Mysterio, 27 – The Pilot, 29 – Smile, 19 – Thin Ice, 10 – Knock Knock, 17 – Oxygen, 33 – Extremis, 12 –The Pyramid at the End of the World, 5 – The Lie of the Land, 1 – Empress of Mars, 31 – The Eaters of Light, 3 – World Enough and Time, 36 – The Doctor Falls

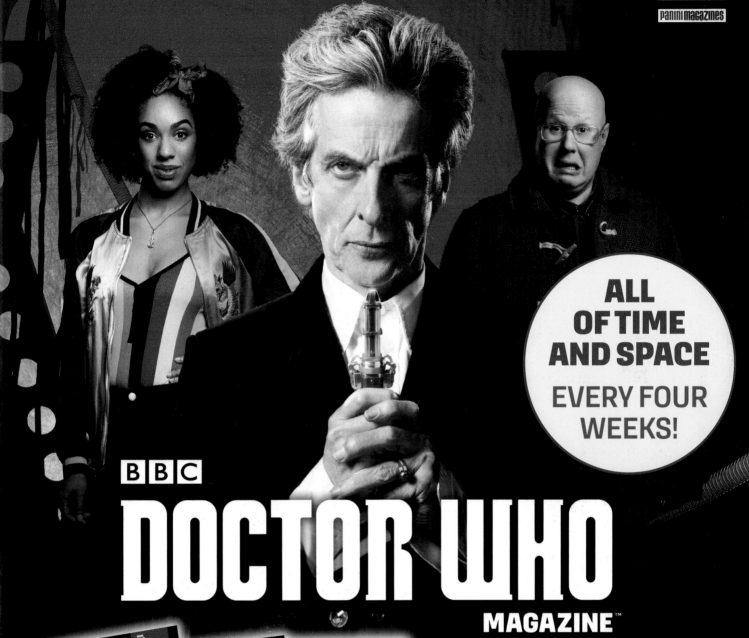

Winning?

Is that what you think it's about?
I'm not trying to win. I'm not doing this because
I want to beat someone . . . or because I hate
someone or because I want to blame someone.
It's not because it's fun. God knows it's not
because it's easy. It's not even because it
works, because it hardly ever does. I do what I
do because it's right! Because it's decent. And,
above all, it's kind. It's just that. Just kind.

If I run away today, good people will die.
If I stand and fight, some of them might live.
Maybe not many, maybe not for long. Hey, maybe
there's no point in any of this at all, but it's the
best I can do. And I will stand here doing it until
it kills me. You're going to die, too, someday.
When will that be? Have you thought about it?
What would you die for?

**Who I am is where I stand.
Where I stand is where I fall.**